CLEVELAND, THE DISCO KING

TO MIKE, MILO,
MARLON, AND MY
DISCO KING,
PATRICIO

Library of Congress Cataloging in Publication Data

Greene, Vivian.
  Cleveland, the disco king.

  SUMMARY: Cleveland has a crush on Odessa
and in order to get her attention and make her like
him, he decides to become a fancy dancer.
  [1. Disco dancing—Fiction] I. Title.
PZ7.G8436C   [E]   79-13057
ISBN 0-531-02513-6
ISBN 0-531-04095-X lib. bdg.

CLEVELAND, THE DISCO KING

BY
VIVIAN GREENE

FRANKLIN WATTS/NEW YORK/LONDON/TORONTO/1979

Cleveland had a crush on Odessa. Girls used to make him sick. But with Odessa it was different. In fact, all he could think about was Odessa.

Cleveland didn't care when his friends teased him. He thought of Odessa's smile. Cleveland didn't care when he couldn't concentrate. He thought of the way she danced. No matter what he was doing, or where he was going, all Cleveland could think about was Odessa.

"Hey," shouted Avalanche as Cleveland ran into her. "What's wrong with you?"

She wondered why Cleveland was acting so strange.

"Going to the disco party Saturday afternoon?"
"A disco party! That's perfect!" said Cleveland.
When Odessa saw him dance, she would fall for
him for sure. Cleveland was so excited he could
hardly wait. If only Saturday would hurry and come.
   He danced pretty well already. And by Saturday
he would be the "Disco King!"

"See you there, honey," said
Cleveland, as he jived away.
"Honey?" said Avalanche.
"I wonder what's got into him?"

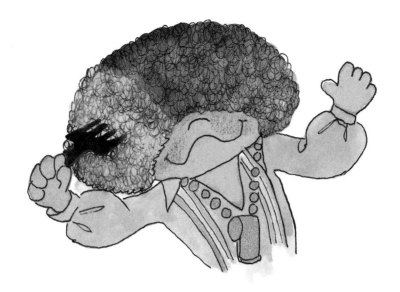

First, I'll get some funky disco clothes, decided Cleveland. Like suspenders and sparkles. And, of course, a disco whistle! And disco hair! He fluffed his Afro and streaked food coloring in his hair.

Then he popped his comb into his back pocket for that finishing touch.

I'll walk real cool, he thought.
He practiced his disco walk.
Odessa will flip! He smiled to himself.

All his friends thought *he'd* flipped.

"Hey, Montgomery!" said Cleveland. "Ready for the disco party?"

"What did you do to yourself?"

"I'm going to be the Disco King," smiled Cleveland. "Odessa will flip!"

"Why don't you try just being yourself?" suggested Montgomery. "Odessa doesn't like all that slick stuff."

But Cleveland wouldn't listen. It was time to go home to watch "Soul Train."

Every day Cleveland practiced and watched and wondered if Saturday would ever come. Of course, it finally did.

Cleveland strode into the party. Wait until Odessa catches this act! he thought. He walked right past her and gave Rotunda the once-over.

Rotunda ate a cookie.
Cleveland hooked his
thumbs in his jeans.
    "Dance?"

"Me?" said Rotunda, a little surprised. She wondered why
Cleveland had colors in his hair. "Uh…sure. I guess," said
Rotunda. Everyone was watching them—even Odessa.

"Freak out!" yelled Cleveland, and got down on his knees.

Rotunda looked scared.

"You don't Freak?" asked Cleveland, who noticed that he was dancing alone. Rotunda shook her head.

"How about the Rock?" he said, swiftly changing step.

Rotunda shook her head.

"The Spank?" he tried. "The Worm?"

Rotunda looked lost. And Odessa
looked worried.

"Take it easy," said Odessa. "Rotunda's
better at the Hustle."

"Great!" said Cleveland, and he spun Rotunda around till they both fell to the floor.

"Are you all right?" cried Odessa, rushing to help Rotunda.
"Good thing I had a lot of cookies back here to soften the fall," joked Rotunda, patting her seat.

Cleveland looked up at Odessa. Here was his chance.

"C'mon, Odessa! You really know how to dance. Let's show 'em!"

"Not now," said Odessa. "Look! Everyone is doing the Bus Stop. Let's join the line."

Cleveland was miserable. Odessa wasn't dying to dance with him. Well, he'd show her. He joined the others and fell right into step.

"This is fun!" said Rotunda, as they clapped to the right.

Everyone was having a good time.

"How about a Soul Train?" suggested Cleveland.

"All right!" said Avalanche, and did her walk through the line.

"Right on!" shouted Cleveland, trying to catch Odessa's eye. He did some splits, two cartwheels, and a karate kick.

"Ouch!" cried Odessa. He'd kicked her!
Of all people!

"Are you okay?" asked Avalanche.

"Let me help you up," said Montgomery.

"That dumb Cleveland!" said Chip.

"I'm okay," said Odessa. "But I think
I'd like to go home."

"I'll go with you," said Rotunda.

"Gee, I'm...a...sorry," said Cleveland.

"Go away!" said Rotunda. "Show-off!"

Cleveland wanted to leave the party, too. Some party. Some Disco King. He felt more like a Disco Dunce.
Odessa would never like him now.

He waited while the girls got their coats. He didn't feel like dancing. He didn't even feel like living.

"Want your jacket?" someone asked. Cleveland looked up.

Odessa! I didn't even think you'd talk to me!
I'll be okay.
I'm not hurt
you're not?

"You didn't? I wasn't. I mean I'm not. I mean...."

"I thought you were a good dancer, too..." started Odessa.

"You did?" asked Cleveland.

"I mean before, when you danced regular."

"Before?" asked Cleveland.

"When we were goofing around at school," she said.

"You noticed?" Cleveland couldn't believe his ears.

Odessa blushed a little. "Yeah, I like to dance like that."

"You do?" Cleveland thought he would burst.

"Do you suppose we could have one last dance before you leave?" Odessa looked unsure. "Nothing fancy, I promise," said Cleveland. "Just like at school."

So they danced one last dance. Odessa
whispered something in Cleveland's ear.
And do you know what?

Odessa had a crush
on Cleveland, too—
all along!